The Ugly Egg

LOU KUENZLER

Illustrated by
DAVID HITCH

To Lily and Isabel, always hatching your own stories,
love Mum - LK
In memory of Rose - DH

KINGFISHER

First published by Kingfisher 2009
an imprint of Macmillan Children's Books
a division of Macmillan Publishers Limited
20 New Wharf Road, London N1 9RR
Basingstoke and Oxford
Associated companies throughout the world
www.panmacmillan.com

ISBN: 978-0-7534-1763-8

Text copyright © Lou Kuenzler 2009
Illustrations copyright © David Hitch 2009

The moral right of the author and illustrator has been asserted.

2 4 6 8 10 9 7 5 3 1
1TR/1108/WKT/SC/115GSM

A CIP catalogue record for this book is available from the British Library.

Printed in China

Contents

Chapter One

WHOOSH! The Arctic wind blew,

straight from the North Pole.

Posy the little puffin shivered.

"Brrrrrrrr! I'm cold!"

"Stay on your nest," warned the

Snow Goose from her rock, high above. "Keep your eggs warm!"

"I don't have any eggs," said Posy.

"No eggs?" said the Snow Goose. "But this is a nest site. *Everyone* here has eggs!"

5

Posy looked around. The Snow Goose was right. All the other birds were sitting on nests. All the other birds had eggs to keep warm.

"I tried to lay an egg," said Posy. "But I couldn't."

"Nonsense!" said the Snow Goose. "Laying an egg is easy. Watch me!"

"Follow her *eggs*ample!" laughed black-and-white Mrs Loon.

The Snow Goose wiggled her tail.

POP!

Out came a snow-white egg.

"See! It's simple!" The Snow Goose peered down at Posy. "I've laid six eggs already," she boasted. This new one makes . . . seven! A fine brood." Posy wished the Snow Goose would stop showing off.

"I'd be happy with one egg," she said to herself. "Just one egg of my own!"

Chapter Two

"Walk in a circle," said the bossy Snow Goose. "That will help you lay an egg." "All right," said Posy. "I'll give it a try."

Round Posy went.

But no egg came.

"Bob up and down!" said Mrs Loon.

"That's what I always do."

Posy bobbed up and down.

"Again!" said the Snow Goose.

"Again!"

Up and down went Posy.

But no egg came.

"Wiggle your bum!" giggled Mrs Loon.

"Wiggle it from side to side!"

Cha-cha-cha!

Posy wiggled her bum.

She wiggled it round and round.

Cha Cha Cha

But still no egg came.

"Don't give up!" said Mrs Loon. "You've nearly cracked it! You'll see!"

Posy shook her head. "It's no good," she said. "I just can't lay an egg."

Posy tucked her head under her wing. She didn't want the others to see her cry.

After a while, she looked up. A shape
caught her eye . . . something big and
oval, out on the ice.

"What's that?" she said.

"It's only an old rock," said the Snow
Goose.

"That's not a rock," said Posy.

"That's an egg!"

Chapter Three

Posy was right.

It was an egg.

An ENORMOUS egg – as big as a

walrus.

It was lumpy. And bumpy. And green.

Dark green with pink spots.

"That is the ugliest egg I have ever seen," said the Snow Goose.

"Ugly egg!" screeched a flock of seagulls.

Posy pressed her head against the lumpy shell. "Don't be mean!" she said. "If there's a chick inside, it will hear you!"

"A good thing too!" said the Snow Goose. "We don't want that egg round here. It's too big and too ugly!"

"Ugly egg! Ugly egg!" screeched the gulls.

"You should be ashamed of yourselves!" said Posy.

She flew gently on to the top of the big, green egg.

"This egg is all alone!" said Posy. "There is no one to keep it warm. I will sit on it until it hatches."

The gulls circled high above Posy and
laughed.

"You're wasting your time with that
ugly old thing," said the Snow Goose.

19

But Posy took no notice.

For three long, cold weeks, Posy sat on the egg.

WHOOSH! The Arctic wind blew, straight from the North Pole.

It blew so hard it nearly knocked Posy off the egg. But Posy held on tight. A cold egg will never hatch. Posy had to keep the egg warm.

She spread her little wings as wide as she could. She hugged the lumpy shell. Posy shivered. Puffins normally lay their eggs deep underground where it is warm. But the huge spotty egg was far too big to bury in a burrow.

Posy didn't mind. She loved the ugly egg! Even when her orange feet turned blue with cold, she didn't move.

"I wonder what is inside this egg" she said.

It was too big to be a puffin. Or a gull. Or even a snow goose.

CRACK!

"Whatever it is," said the Snow Goose, "that horrible egg is about to hatch!"

Chapter Four

There was a sound like ice breaking.

"Look out!" hissed the Snow Goose.

CRACK!

A big webbed foot slipped out of the

egg.

Out flopped a pair of folded wings.
They were red. And smooth. And
shiny . . .

"There's not a feather on them!" cried
the Snow Goose.

"It's naked!" screeched the gulls.

"Shhh!" said Posy. "Don't frighten
him!"

Crack! *Crack!*

Out came a long, thick tail.

"Ugly monster!" hissed the Snow Goose. "It's not a bird at all!"

"It must be a bird," said a seagull. "It came out of an egg."

The Snow Goose flapped her wings.

"That *thing* is NOT a bird," she said.

"*Eggs*traordinary!" said Mrs Loon.

"What is it?" screeched the gulls.

25

Posy pushed away the broken eggshell. "Can't you see?" she said. "He's a dragon! A beautiful baby dragon!"

Chapter Five

The dragon staggered to his feet.

"He's so cute!" said Posy.

SNORT!

FLASH!

Flames shot from the dragon's nose.

"If he's going to breathe fire," said Mrs Loon, "you ought to call him . . . Burney!"

"Burney?" said Posy. "I like that name!"

Burney seemed to like his name too.

SNORT!

FLASH!

He blew another flame.

"Get that monster away from here,"
hissed the Snow Goose.

"He'll burn our nests with his fiery
breath," cried a gull.

"He'll eat our chicks with his terrible
jaws," warned another.

"Shoo! Shoo!" screeched all the gulls together.

"Don't let Burney burn our nests," they cried.

The Snow Goose and the gulls flew at the baby dragon. From all across the nest site angry birds came.

"Stop!" cried Posy.

But the birds wouldn't listen.

They flapped their wings. They pecked. They dived. They swooped at the little dragon.

"They're all in a flap!" cried Mrs Loon.

"Shoo, monster! Shoo!" shrieked the gulls.

Birds plunged. Feathers flew!

WHIRL!

SWIRL!

The wind blew up a storm of snow and
feathers.

The birds lunged at Burney again.

They jabbed him with their sharp

claws and beaks.

"Stop!" begged Posy.

But Burney fled.

"Hooray!" cheered the Snow
Goose. "We've scared the monster
away!"

Chapter Six

Posy flew above the nest site.

"Burney," she called. "Burney, where are you?"

Posy flew out over the deep, cold sea. She flapped high over the steep grey cliffs, then back over the nest site again.

"Burney's only a baby. He's too young
to be alone," she cried.

"And he's too dangerous," said the
Snow Goose.

"THERE HE IS!" screeched the gulls.

The dragon pup was high on the rocks.

He was crouched beside the Snow

Goose's nest.

"He's eating my eggs," shrieked the
Snow Goose. "He'll fry them with
his breath. He'll gobble them for
breakfast!"

"That's not true," said
Posy. "Look! He isn't
eating your eggs . . .
He's keeping them
warm!"

In all the fuss, the careless Snow Goose had forgotten to stay on her nest. She had left her eggs alone in the snow. They were getting cold.

WHOOSH! The Arctic wind blew, straight from the North Pole.

But Burney breathed gently.

Puff!

He blew tiny flames of warmth across
the nest.

"My eggs are starting to hatch!" said
the Snow Goose.

The dragon blew gently again.

Puff! Puff!

Seven tiny goslings poked their heads out of the nest.

Posy and Mrs Loon cheered.

"My babies!" The Snow Goose flew close to the dragon.

"I'm sorry," she said. "I was wrong about you, Burney. You're not a monster. You saved my eggs. You kept them warm."

Burney blew a perfect purple smoke ring. And he bowed.

"He's so warm-hearted," giggled Mrs Loon.

Everyone gathered around the nest.

That night the Snow Goose was happy
with her seven new goslings.

And Posy had her baby
dragon to look after.

She snuggled under Burney's fiery chin.
WHOOSH! The Arctic wind blew,
straight from the North Pole.
But Posy had never felt so warm in all
her life.

About the Author and Illustrator

Lou Kuenzler grew up on a sheep farm in Devon. She now lives in London with one husband, two children, two cats and one dog. Lou teaches drama to children and grown ups. But, best of all, she likes to write stories. Lou says, "It's a bit like sitting on a big egg and waiting to see what will hatch!"

David Hitch studied illustration at Central St Martins in London where he still lives with his partner. He has been illustrating for over 15 years. David says "just like the dragon hatching the eggs, I like to breathe life into stories with my illustrations."

Tips for Beginner Readers

1. Think about the cover and the title of the book. What do you think it will be about? While you are reading, think about what might happen next and why.

2. As you read, ask yourself if what you're reading makes sense. If it doesn't, try rereading or look at the pictures for clues.

3. If there is a word that you do not know, look carefully at the letters, sounds and word parts that you do know. Blend the sounds to read the word. Is this a word you know? Does it make sense in the sentence?

4. Think about the characters, where the story takes place, and the problems the characters in the story faced. What are the important ideas in the beginning, middle and end of the story?

5. Ask yourself questions like:
Did you like the story?
Why or why not?
How did the author make it fun to read?
How well did you understand it?

Maybe you can understand the story better if you read it again!